W9-BLZ-171

Dear Parents:

Congratulations! Your child is taking the first steps on an exciting journey. The destination? Independent reading!

STEP INTO READING® will help your child get there. The program offers five steps to reading success. Each step includes fun stories and colorful art or photographs. In addition to original fiction and books with favorite characters, there are Step into Reading Non-Fiction Readers, Phonics Readers and Boxed Sets, Sticker Readers, and Comic Readers—a complete literacy program with something to interest every child.

Learning to Read, Step by Step!

Ready to Read   Preschool–Kindergarten
• big type and easy words • rhyme and rhythm • picture clues
For children who know the alphabet and are eager to begin reading.

Reading with Help   Preschool–Grade 1
• basic vocabulary • short sentences • simple stories
For children who recognize familiar words and sound out new words with help.

Reading on Your Own   Grades 1–3
• engaging characters • easy-to-follow plots • popular topics
For children who are ready to read on their own.

Reading Paragraphs   Grades 2–3
• challenging vocabulary • short paragraphs • exciting stories
For newly independent readers who read simple sentences with confidence.

Ready for Chapters   Grades 2–4
• chapters • longer paragraphs • full-color art
For children who want to take the plunge into chapter books but still like colorful pictures.

STEP INTO READING® is designed to give every child a successful reading experience. The grade levels are only guides; children will progress through the steps at their own speed, developing confidence in their reading.

Remember, a lifetime love of reading starts with a single step!

Step into Reading, Random House, and the Random House colophon are registered trademarks
of Penguin Random House LLC.

Visit us on the Web!
StepIntoReading.com
rhcbooks.com

Educators and librarians, for a variety of teaching tools, visit us at RHTeachersLibrarians.com

ISBN 978-0-7364-4197-1 (trade) — ISBN 978-0-7364-9004-7 (lib. bdg.)
ISBN 978-0-7364-4198-8 (ebook)

Printed in the United States of America   10 9 8 7 6 5 4 3 2 1

Disney · PIXAR

LUCA

A Sea Monster Story

adapted by Natasha Bouchard

illustrated by the Disney Storybook Art Team

Random House 🏠 New York

Luca is a sea monster.

He lives in the ocean.

Luca is curious about the world
above the surface.
His parents say it is dangerous.
Land monsters hunt sea monsters!

Luca follows a trail
of human objects.
It leads him to another
sea monster named Alberto.

Alberto lives on land.

Luca follows him to the surface.

Sea monsters turn into humans
when they are not in water.

Alberto has a hideout

filled with human stuff.

Luca sees a scooter poster.

He imagines riding one.

Luca and Alberto try

to build their own scooter.

When Luca returns home,
his mom scolds him for being late.
Luca's grandma makes up
an excuse for him.

The next day, Luca
returns to see Alberto.
They have fun trying
out their wobbly scooter.

Luca's parents are worried.
They do not want Luca
going up to the surface
ever again.
They will send him far away
to live with his Uncle Ugo.

Luca does not want to go.

He runs away.

Luca and Alberto

escape to Portorosso.

The human world is exciting!

But it is dangerous

for sea monsters.

Luca and Alberto are careful

to keep their secret.

They spot a shiny scooter.

It belongs to Ercole.

He is the champion

of the Portorosso Cup race.

Ercole pushes Luca into a fountain.

Luca begins to transform!

A human girl named Giulia
stands up for Luca.
Luca and Alberto convince Giulia
to enter the Portorosso Cup race
with them.

Luca and Alberto want
to buy a scooter with
the prize money.
But first, they have to train
for the race.
Alberto must learn to eat
lots of pasta.

Luca must learn to ride a bike.

During their training,

Giulia talks about her school.

Luca wants to go to school, too.

Alberto feels left out.

Alberto is jealous.

He jumps onto Luca's bike

and they speed down a hill.

Luca and Alberto

struggle for control.

They crash into the sea!

Luca and Alberto argue.

Alberto reveals to Giulia

that he is a sea monster.

Luca pretends to be surprised.

Luca is sorry.

He wants to make amends
with Alberto.

Luca will race on his own.

He promises to win the race
and buy a new scooter for them.

The Portorosso Cup race
is about to begin!
The racers get ready
at the starting line.

They're off!
First, they swim
a lap in the ocean.

Next, they eat heaps of pasta.

Giulia feels sick.

Ercole cheats.

Luca is the last to finish.

Finally, it is time for the bike race.

Luca is doing great!

But it starts to rain.

He must take shelter.

Alberto comes to help Luca.

Alberto gets wet and transforms

into a sea monster.

Alberto is trapped in a net.

Luca rides out into the rain

to rescue him.

Now Luca transforms, too.

Their secret is out!

Just as Ercole closes in on them,

Giulia crashes into Ercole!

She is hurt.

Alberto and Luca

jump off their bike

and run back to help her.

Luca stands up to Ercole.

He is not afraid anymore.

Luca and Alberto
crossed the finish line
without realizing it.
They have won the race!

Luca and Alberto
buy their scooter.
Everyone celebrates
their victory.

Alberto helps Luca go to school.

He sells the scooter to buy

Luca a train ticket.

Luca wants Alberto to come, too.

But Alberto wants

to stay in Portorosso.

Luca says goodbye.
He boards the train
and heads off for his
next adventure.